# THE SCAR

Charlotte Moundlic • illustrated by Olivier Tallec

CANDLEWICK PRESS

Original text and artwork copyright © Père Castor/Éditions Flammarion, 2009. Originally published in France as *La Croûte*. Translation copyright © 2011 Candlewick Press. All rights reserved. First U.S. edition 2011. Library of Congress Cataloging-in-Publication Data is available. Library of Congress Catalog Card Number 2010042792. ISBN 978-0-7636-5341-5. Printed in Humen, Dongguan, China. This book was typeset in Alghera. The illustrations were done in acrylic and pencil. Candlewick Press, 99 Dover Street, Somerville, Massachusetts 02144. Visit us at www.candlewick.com. 11 12 13 14 15 16 SCP 10 9 8 7 6 5 4 3 2 1

Mom died this morning.
It wasn't really this morning.
Dad said she died during the night,
but I was sleeping during the night.
For me, she died this morning.

Yesterday, my mom was still alive. She lay in her bed and smiled a little, and she told me that she would love me all her life but that she was too tired, that her body couldn't carry her anymore, and that she was going away forever.
I told her that she could come back after she was rested, that I would wait for her.

She said that she wished she could but that it wasn't possible.
Her smile got smaller and her eyes were a bit wet.
That made me mad, and I shouted that if it was going to be like that, I wouldn't be her son anymore, that she shouldn't have had a kid if she was going to leave before he was grown up.

She laughed a bit, but I cried, because I knew that she was really going to die.

When I woke up this morning, everything was quiet. I couldn't smell coffee or hear the radio. I came downstairs, and my dad said, "Is that you, honey?"

I thought that was a silly question, because other than Mom, who was too sick to get out of bed anymore, and Dad, who was the one asking the question, I was the only one in the house.

I said, "No, no, it's not me," which I thought was pretty funny, but then I noticed that Dad wasn't laughing. He smiled a very small smile, and said, "It's over," and I pretended I didn't understand.

Dad said, "She's gone forever."

I knew that she wasn't *gone* — she was dead and I would never see her again. They were going to put her in a box and then in the ground, where she would turn into dust.

I know very well that dying means that you're never going to come back.

"Well, good riddance!" I yelled to Dad. I couldn't believe she'd left us. How will Dad know how to make my toast the way I like it, cut in half with the honey in a zigzag? I was sure that Mom didn't teach him how, and now it's too late. He won't be able to manage without her.

Luckily, I'm still here, and I can explain everything to Dad.
I told him, "Don't worry. I'll take care of you."
And I cried a little because I didn't really know how
to take care of a dad who's been abandoned like this.
I could tell that he'd been crying, too —
he looked like a washcloth, all crumpled and wet.
I don't really like seeing Dad cry.

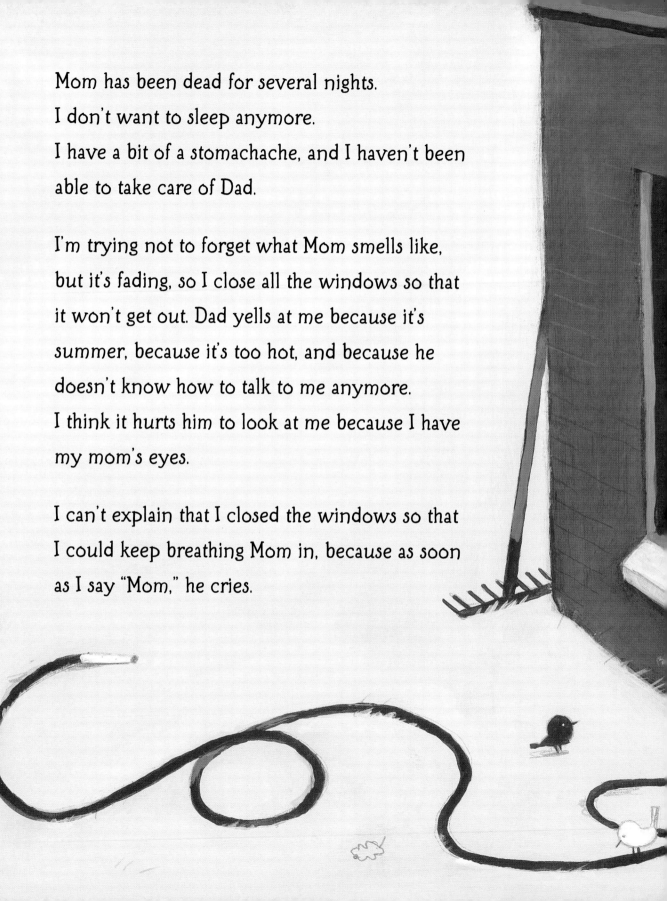

Mom has been dead for several nights.
I don't want to sleep anymore.
I have a bit of a stomachache, and I haven't been
able to take care of Dad.

I'm trying not to forget what Mom smells like,
but it's fading, so I close all the windows so that
it won't get out. Dad yells at me because it's
summer, because it's too hot, and because he
doesn't know how to talk to me anymore.
I think it hurts him to look at me because I have
my mom's eyes.

I can't explain that I closed the windows so that
I could keep breathing Mom in, because as soon
as I say "Mom," he cries.

It's not just Mom's smell that's fading — I feel like I can barely remember the sound of her voice. So I plug my ears, cover my eyes, and shut my mouth to keep it with me. (But not my nose, because I need to breathe.)

All my life, whenever I hurt myself, Mom would tell me,
"It's just a scratch, my little man. You're too strong
for anything to hurt you." I would close my eyes
and she'd open her arms to me, and the pain would
disappear like that.

Yesterday, I fell while I was running on the garden wall, and I got a big scrape on my knee, which wasn't much fun, but I heard it — my mother's voice. So something good came out of my getting hurt. I waited until a little scab formed and I scratched it so that it opened again and the blood came back. It hurt a bit and I tried not to cry.

I told myself that as long as there was blood, I would still hear my mom's voice. And I would be a little less sad.

This morning, Grandma showed up.
She's my mom's mom.

I'm a bit worried, because now I have two
sad adults to take care of. And on top of that,
I've got to keep an eye on my scab.

At first, Grandma hardly moves, but then she starts looking around our house like she's searching for something or someone. She can't sit still, and the last straw is when she opens the windows wide.

"It's too hot in this house. We're all going to suffocate," she says.

And that's too much for me. I shout and cry and scream, "No! Don't open the windows! Mom's going to disappear for good. . . ." And I fall and the tears flow without stopping, and there's nothing I can do and I feel very tired.

I'm scared that Grandma will think I'm crazy.
But no, she comes close to me and puts her
hand, then my hand, on my heart.

"She's there," she says, "in your heart, and she's
not going anywhere."

I feel better after Grandma tells me that. She's older than I am, and she's my mom's mom, so she should know.

I'm so afraid of forgetting Mom completely that once I know that she's in my heart, whenever I can, I run. I run until my muscles hurt, until it hurts to breathe. And then I feel Mom beating very hard in my chest.

Grandma showed Dad how to make the honey zigzag, but he isn't very good at it. I don't say anything, since I have to encourage him if I want him to make progress.

Grandma went home a few days ago, and when I woke
up this morning, I smelled coffee and heard a voice on the
radio saying that it was going to be a nice day.

"It's me!" I shout from the top of the stairs, which is dumb,
since Dad knows that we're the only two here, but it
makes him smile.

He opens his arms to me, I throw myself in them, and my
heart beats so hard I can almost hear Mom whispering,
"Go on, my little man. Go on. . . ."

In bed tonight, I brush my knee with the tip of my finger,
and the skin is all smooth, all new. I kick back my covers
and look more closely and see that the scab is gone.
It's turned into a scar without me noticing.
For a second I think I might cry, but I don't.

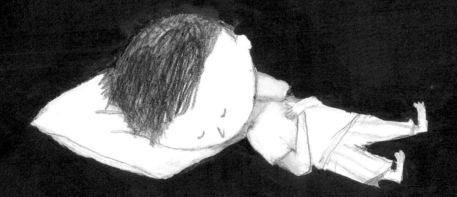

I lie back, my hands on my chest. My heart beats quietly, peacefully, and it lulls me to sleep.